For Lucas — AF

For my Foxy family —

STRIPES PUBLISHING
An imprint of Little Tiger Press
1 The Coda Centre, 189 Munster Road,
London SW6 6AW

A paperback original
First published in Great Britain in 2015

ISBN: 978-1-84715-616-7

Fox Investigates

A Brush with Danger

ADAM FROST
ILLUSTRATED BY EMILY FOX

Stripes

IT STARTS WITH A BANG!

It was nine o'clock in the morning and the Wily Fox Detective Agency was open for business. Already there was a long queue of animals waiting outside – sheep, mice, owls, ocelots, ostriches and more.

Inside, Wily was sitting at his desk, polishing his favourite magnifying glass with his bushy tail. He glanced up at the clock, put his magnifying glass in a drawer and pressed a button on the desk.

"Send in the first client, Mrs Mongoose," he said into a small microphone.

"Certainly, Mr Fox," replied a crackly voice.

"I hope something good turns up today," Wily murmured to himself. "If I hear another case of a squirrel who can't find his nuts, I'll—"

At that moment, there was a loud scream followed by an enormous…

Wily leaped to his feet and sprinted across the office.

Outside in reception, it was chaos. There was smoke everywhere and animals were scrambling up the walls, leaping out of windows and sprinting down the stairs.

Mrs Mongoose was flapping her arms, shouting, "Please leave the building in an orderly fashion."

Wily was about to dash downstairs when the smoke parted, the screaming stopped and a slinky silhouette came slowly into the room.

The detective rubbed his eyes and blinked twice. The silhouette became an elegant young poodle with large brown eyes and soft black fur. She had a red beret perched on one side of her head.

"Fireworks can come in very handy," she purred in a French accent, waving an empty box of bangers. "I hope you don't mind me – how you say – *pushing in*," she added.

Wily gave a half-smile. "No problem. That was quite a neat trick. I might use it myself some time."

7

"Dogs like to do tricks," said the poodle. "Perhaps I will teach you some others. But for now, the show is over."

She walked through the empty reception, smiling at a surprised-looking Mrs Mongoose, and passed into Wily's office.

"It's OK, Mrs Mongoose," Wily said. "I'll take it from here." He sat down at his desk and the poodle started to speak.

"My name is Suzie La Pooch. I own one of the greatest art galleries in Paris. Inside there are some of the most famous paintings in the world. See for yourself..."

Self-Pawtrait

Dark Bones

"Fascinating, Mademoiselle, but I am a detective, not an art critic," Wily said, snapping the catalogue shut. "Why should this interest me?"

"Because I have fallen in love with the wrong painting," said Suzie.

Wily blinked. "OK..."

"Two weeks ago, I bought a painting from a gallery owned by a brown bear from Russia called Dimitri Gottabottomitch. The picture was small, a bit strange-looking, but I LOVED it. A day later, I got a phone call."

"From who?" Wily asked.

"It was Dimitri. He said the gallery assistant had made a mistake. The painting wasn't for sale. He wanted it back."

"So – let me guess – you refused?"

"Of course I did. I'd fallen in love. I offered him more money – ten times what I'd paid – but he

kept saying it wasn't for sale. Then he called me rude names. Well, that did it. Nobody is rude to Suzie La Pooch. I hung up."

"That's odd behaviour for a businessman," Wily muttered. "Refusing ten times the asking price."

"Yesterday, this arrived," said Suzie. She handed Wily a note:

> THIS IS YOUR LAST CHANCE.
> GIVE ME BACK MY PAINTING,
> OR THINGS WILL GET NASTY.

Wily looked at the handwriting. Then he smelled the paper. He thought he recognized the scent – there was brown bear, but also something else...

"I must admit, this note unsettled me," Suzie said. "I closed my gallery to the public.

Locked the door. Turned on the alarms. Flew straight to London and came here."

Wily looked up. "I assume giving the painting back is not an option."

Suzie shook her head. "First, he is rude. Now, he is making threats. I may be a poodle on the outside, but inside I am pure Rottweiler."

"And you don't want to contact the police?"

"What if they take Dimitri's side? Tell me to give the painting back," said Suzie. "Besides, police officers are not very clever. I want to keep the painting and I want to know why Dimitri wants it back so badly. It seems that there's something rather strange behind it all."

"True," said Wily. "OK, I'll take the case. Return to your gallery at once and I'll follow on. You may have locks and alarms, but Dimitri will have crowbars and drills. We need to make the place a fortress. Then we'll work out why the painting is so special."

"*Merci*, Monsieur Fox," said Suzie, "I knew I could count on you. See you in Paris this afternoon."

The poodle picked up her catalogue and walked out.

Wily pressed another button on his desk. The speaker crackled. "Did you get all that, Albert?" he asked.

A squeaky voice replied, "Of course."

"Good," said Wily. "I'm on my way down."

He walked over to a bookcase and pulled out a copy of *Fantastic Mr Fox*. The bookcase slid across to reveal a fireman's pole that was at least a mile long.

Wily put on a pair of gloves and thigh pads that were hanging on the wall. Then he leaped on to the pole and started to hurtle downwards. After a couple of minutes, Wily gripped with the thigh pads to slow his pace. He landed with a soft *pouf* on a crash mat in the middle of an underground laboratory.

"Morning, Albert," said Wily. "What have you got for me today?"

A small mole with huge glasses emerged from the shadows.

"So, I hear you're going to Paris…" He yanked a piece of rope that was under his arm, and a curtain whipped aside to reveal a moped.

"This is called a Vespa," he said. "Everyone there has one. However, yours is slightly different." The mole pulled a lever on the side of the bike and a gigantic rocket slid out of the back.

13

"It can fly," Albert said proudly.

He pulled another lever and a large corkscrew popped out of the front. "And it digs tunnels."

He pointed at a third lever. "And if you pull that, it turns into a submarine."

"Wow," said Wily. "Anything else?"

"Actually, there is," said Albert. "If you whistle, it will come to you. Within a distance of a hundred metres. And if you tap that screen, you can talk to me at any time."

Wily smiled. "Does it serve coffee, too?"

"Er, actually, no," Albert apologized. "I didn't, er, think about that..."

"I'm only joking, Albert," said Wily. "It's brilliant!" He climbed on. "Now, show me how this rocket works. I have to be in Paris by midday."

A KNOCKOUT PRESENT

Wily was standing in Suzie's gallery, La Pooch of Paris. The walls were white and bare with pale grey squares every couple of metres.

"Where are all the paintings?" he asked.

Suzie smiled. "I had this installed earlier this year. Now I'm very glad I did."

She took out a remote control from her pocket and pressed a red button. There was a whirring noise and the grey squares flipped round to reveal Suzie's paintings.

"Clever," Wily said. "Dimitri doesn't stand

a chance. Now, which one does he want back?"

Suzie glided over to a small painting at the end of the room. "This one," she said.

It certainly was a very strange-looking painting. Wily looked at the description underneath: 'Vole Inspecting a Nervous Woodlouse' by Kandogski.

"Incredible, isn't it?" said Suzie. "It works on so many levels. Every time you look at it, you find something new."

"It's certainly … different," said Wily, looking around at the other paintings in Suzie's gallery.

"That's why I'm so excited," said Suzie. "Kandogski is a new discovery."

At that moment, they heard a knock. Suzie pressed a button on the remote control and the paintings flipped round, leaving the walls bare.

"Stay hidden," said Wily. "I'll see who it is."

The detective moved slowly towards the door, ready to unleash one of his kung-fu moves. He put his paw on the handle and opened it a fraction. He couldn't see anyone. He opened it a fraction more.

A squirrel darted in and looked at Wily in surprise. "Wily! What are you doing here?"

The squirrel was in police uniform and her name badge read: SYBIL SQUIRREL, JUNIOR DETECTIVE, PSSST (Police Spy, Sleuth and Snoop Taskforce).

"Sybil!" Wily exclaimed. "I might ask you the same question!"

"The French government got in touch," Sybil explained. "The La Pooch gallery suddenly closed its doors to the public. No warning. No explanation given. It looked fishy."

"Well, it isn't," Wily insisted.

"Oh yeah," Sybil said with a grin. "What are *you* doing here, then?"

A second later, she was barged out of the way by an angry-looking bulldog.

"Wily Fox!" he barked. "I might have known."

"Julius Hound," Wily replied, with a mock bow.

"Give me three good reasons why I shouldn't arrest you for tampering with a crime scene," said Julius.

Suzie La Pooch moved forward. "Because this isn't a crime scene, Monsieur. It's my gallery and I invited Mr Fox here," she said.

For a split second, Julius stopped in his tracks, staring at the elegant poodle, but he swiftly recovered. "I don't know what he's told you, Mademoiselle, but if you've got a problem, you should have come to me – the head of PSSST – not this meddling twerp."

"I don't have a problem," Suzie said. "Mr Fox is a dear friend of mine."

Julius looked around at the bare walls of the gallery and back at Suzie. "If you don't have a problem, then where are all your paintings?"

Suzie blinked. "They're safe."

"Not stolen?"

"Not stolen."

"I don't believe you."

"I don't care," said Suzie.

"Prove it or I'll arrest you."

Suzie sighed. "Fine. Arrest me."

Suzie held out her arms, waiting for the handcuffs. There was a tense silence. Then a knock on the door made everyone jump.

Wily moved towards it.

"Not you," Julius growled. "Sybil, go and see who's there."

The squirrel opened the door carefully and stepped outside. They heard the muffled sounds of a conversation, and then Sybil reappeared with a parcel.

"Delivery for Miss La Pooch," she said. "Says it's from an admirer. It smells like it's from that posh cheese shop round the corner."

"Give it to me, Sybil," Wily snapped.

"Oh no, you don't," said Julius, standing between Wily and the parcel.

"Don't be a fool, Julius," said Wily. "You don't know who sent it or what's inside."

"And maybe *you* do," said Julius. "Is the

cheese shop in on this plot? Perhaps it contains money? Or a smuggled painting?"

"Julius, do *not* open it," Wily growled.

But Julius was already angrily tearing off the lid of the parcel. "I'll get to the bottom of this," he muttered.

The bulldog put his paw inside the parcel and pulled out a lump of yellow cheese. He frowned, sniffed it and then collapsed on the floor in a heap.

"Oh no!" Wily exclaimed and jumped on top of the cheese, covering it with his body.

"What is it?" cried Sybil.

"It's Le Pong Beaucoup, the smelliest cheese in Paris!" Wily declared. "It knocks you out in seconds. Poisons you in minutes. Get out of here and take Suzie with you!"

Yellow gas was beginning to seep round the edges of Wily's coat.

Sybil grabbed Suzie and headed for a small

door at the back of the gallery. As they ducked through, the main doors of the gallery were forced open and two wolves wearing gas masks rushed inside.

The wolves sniggered at Julius's unconscious body as they stepped over it.

Wily could feel the cheese beginning to fizz and bubble as the gas struggled to escape. The wolves peered down at Wily, who was lying still with his eyes closed.

"He isn't going anywhere," said one.

"He'll be no trouble to us," said the other. They both had thick Russian accents.

The first wolf put a bag of tools down on the ground and pulled out a crowbar.

Wily felt his head beginning to spin. Then he had an idea. "Hmmr phhr mmm," he said.

"What?" said the first wolf.

"Hmmr phdd mmrr," said Wily, beckoning

the wolf towards him.

The wolf leaned over, putting his face right next to Wily's. "What?" he growled.

Quick as a flash, Wily pulled out the cheese, lifted up the wolf's gas mask and shoved the cheese into his mouth. The wolf was so confused, he gulped it down. First he turned red. Then he turned purple.

Finally he ran out of the gallery, yellow steam pouring out of his ears.

Wily jumped to his feet and looked around for the other wolf, but the gallery seemed empty. Then he felt something heavy hit him on the back of the head and everything went black.

Time passed. Wily felt himself being shaken awake. He opened his eyes and saw Suzie leaning over him. He sat up and rubbed his head.

"Is everyone OK?" he asked.

"Julius is talking about pink unicorns, but otherwise everyone is fine," she said.

"And the painting?" asked Wily.

"Not fine," said Suzie. "My Kandogski has gone!"

THE BEAR
WHO WASN'T THERE

Wily was tearing down a long straight boulevard on his Vespa. He tapped the screen between the handlebars.

"Albert? Are you there?" he called.

In an instant, Albert appeared. "I'm here, Wily."

In the background, Wily could see the temporary HQ that the mole had set up in the Paris sewers. "I need your help," said Wily. "I'm heading for Dimitri Gottabottomitch's office, by the Eiffel Tower."

"I thought you were at Suzie's," said Albert.

"I was," said Wily. "Then two wolves broke into the gallery and took Suzie's painting. I was almost killed by some smelly cheese, before being knocked on the head by a... Anyway, enough of that, I've got to find these wolves."

"You think they'll have taken the painting to Dimitri's office?"

"I'm not sure," said Wily. "But I do know that brown bear is responsible for all this."

Wily turned down a side street.

"So *how* did they steal the painting?" asked Albert.

"It's a long story, but basically Julius turned up," said Wily.

"Julius?" said Albert. "PSSST was there? That's odd."

"I know," said Wily. "This case is getting stranger by the minute. And I don't think this is just about a painting, Albert. Those wolves could have stolen every piece in Suzie's gallery. But they just took the Kandogski. That smelly cheese could have killed us. Who commits murder for the sake of a painting?"

"It's weird all right," said Albert. "So what do you need me to do?"

"Find out everything you can about this Kandogski bloke," said Wily. "We need to know what is it that's making Dimitri care so much."

"You got it," said Albert.

Wily turned off the screen. He looked up and saw the Eiffel Tower straight ahead. He parked his scooter and walked the last hundred metres, so no one would hear him coming. When he got close to Dimitri's office, he ducked behind a hedge.

Outside the door, Wily could see a wolf.

In front of the office, there was a van. A young goat dragged a desk into the back and went to sit in the driver's seat.

"Leaving town, Dimitri?" Wily muttered.

The detective knew he had to get closer. He crossed the street, flattened himself against the side of the van and peered inside – there were no paintings, just office equipment. Wily glanced over at the wolf by the door. Then he had an idea.

Wily had always been able to throw his voice. He had caught the notorious Purple Monkey gang by making it sound like their boss, Bruno Baboon, was trapped in a vat of superglue.

Now was a good time to practise his ventriloquism skills.

He put his hand around his snout and shouted, "How did I end up in here?" It sounded like his voice was coming from inside the van.

The wolf looked up.

"Where am I? Help!" Wily called out again.

The wolf immediately ran over and leaped inside the van, looking around in confusion. Wily swiftly closed the doors behind him, and banged on them loudly.

"Ready to go now, driver," he said, in his best Russian accent.

The van revved its engine and sped off. Wily could hear the wolf calling out and banging angrily on the sides.

"That's one out of the way," said Wily.

He crept towards the door of Dimitri's office and sniffed. He could smell wolf and also ... BEAR.

He had no time to lose – he padded quietly into the front office.

It was deserted. There was nothing in the room except a chair in the corner and an empty safe in the wall.

Wily went over to the safe and peered inside. Whatever had been kept in there had been removed.

But then he felt something tickling his feet. He looked down and saw a white triangle of paper sticking out from between the floorboards. In their rush to empty the safe, Dimitri or his wolves must have dropped it on the floor. It had slid between the floorboards, leaving just a tiny corner poking out. Wily grabbed the triangle carefully with his finger and thumb. He pulled out not one, but *three* sheets of paper.

The first read:

The second painting is on its way.

The handwriting looked familiar. Wily knew he had seen it somewhere before. But where?

The second scrap of paper was actually a photo. This was even more of a surprise.

It was a photo taken in his final year at detective school, just before their exams. His friend Klara had taken it and given a copy to everyone there. Rudi Raccoon, Barry Badger, Hildegard Hamster and all his other classmates.

But how had the photo turned up in Dimitri's office? Was one of his friends from detective school helping the Russian bear? It didn't make sense. Who would do this? And why?

He glanced at the third scrap of paper.

CLAUDE'S COURIERS

1 x painting by Kandogski successfully delivered to: Gallery Nouvelle, The Old Docks, Paris, FRANCE

A delivery note. So there *were* other Kandogski paintings. But if Dimitri had sold this Kandogski to Gallery Nouvelle, why didn't he want to sell another one to Suzie?

Wily's head was buzzing with all this new information. Then suddenly he heard a door slam and saw a shape rush past the window.

The detective ran outside.

A brown bear was ambling towards the Eiffel
Tower, holding something that looked like a
rolled-up painting tucked under his arm.

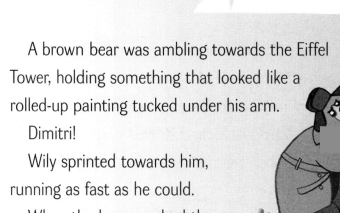

Dimitri!

Wily sprinted towards him,
running as fast as he could.

When the bear reached the
Eiffel Tower, he glanced up and
started to climb, pulling himself
up the metal struts.

Wily didn't think twice. He
climbed, too, bounding up the
side of the tower in strong leaps.

Soon a rumbling noise
started to shake the tower.
The bear looked up and
saw a helicopter hovering
above him. He waved
it over.

Wily didn't have much time. He threw himself on Dimitri's back. But the bear shook him off and kept climbing. Wily jumped again, grabbing Dimitri's foot. This time, the bear lost his grip and fell, landing on Wily's head. They scuffled and Wily grabbed the painting, but Dimitri snatched it back and kept on climbing.

With one final, gigantic effort, Wily hurled himself at Dimitri, yanking the painting from under his arm. The painting unrolled, but it was blank except for the words:

NICE TRY, MR FOX

A rope ladder had been dropped from the helicopter and the bear was now reaching for it. In a rage, Wily jumped and grabbed Dimitri's foot, but this time it fell off! Then Dimitri's legs and back fell off, too, and Wily realized he was holding on to a very convincing bear costume.

"Dimitri?" he asked.

A wolf was clinging to the tower, holding a bear head in his hands. "Not me," he laughed, pointing at the ground. "That is Dimitri."

Wily looked down and saw a bear, carrying a painting, climb into a taxi.

The wolf leaped on to the rope ladder. "I should have killed you at the gallery," he growled, "but then again, this way is much more fun." He threw the bear head down at the detective, knocking Wily off the tower.

Wily fell like a stone towards the ground.

WILY'S SUPER SUB

As he fell, watching the metal girders of the
Eiffel Tower whizz past, Wily remembered
something. Albert had adapted the Vespa so it
would come when he whistled.

Wily tried to whistle, but the air rushing
past his mouth made his lips jiggle. He tried to
whistle again, glancing down at the ground that
was rapidly hurtling towards him. A tiny peep
came out of his lips, but no Vespa appeared.

In desperation, Wily put two fingers in his
mouth and gave the loudest possible fox-whistle

(like a wolf-whistle, but even more ear-piercing). In an alley fifty metres away, the Vespa's rocket roared into life. It shot through the air and caught the fox just before he hit the ground. Wily lay back on the seat, gasping and shuddering, while the Vespa floated in mid-air, waiting for further instructions.

A few seconds passed. Two pigeons hovered next to the detective's head.

"Look, Pierre," one of the pigeons quipped. "A flying fox."

"Hilarious," Wily growled and sat up. He flew the Vespa through the legs of the Eiffel Tower and parked.

He looked up at the sky. The helicopter was gone. He looked at the street. The taxi – with Dimitri and the painting – was gone.

But he was still alive. And now he realized he was something else, too.

Annoyed. Very annoyed.

Wily tapped the screen and Albert appeared. Behind him was a gigantic shelf of books.

"Albert," said Wily, "where are you?"

"In the library," said Albert. "I can't find a single reference to Kandogski. Or a single painting by him, either."

"Hmm, interesting... And there's something else," said Wily. "I think an old friend of mine might be behind all this."

He showed the photograph he'd found in Dimitri's office to Albert and explained that the animals were his classmates at detective school.

"Albert," said Wily, "I need you to cross-reference all the people in this photo to the handwriting up here. Where it says, 'This one's Wily Fox'."

"OK," said the mole. "Slide it across the face of the screen."

Wily did this, and an exact copy emerged from the side of the tablet that Albert was holding.

"Find out which one of these animals wrote that message," said Wily.

"Will do," said Albert.

"And now I need to find out *why* they wrote it," said Wily.

"Be careful, Wily," said Albert.

The screen went black.

Wily pulled out the third piece of paper he had found in Dimitri's office.

CLAUDE'S COURIERS

1 x painting by Kandogski successfully delivered to:
Gallery Nouvelle, The Old Docks, Paris,
FRANCE

"I think it's time to pay Gallery Nouvelle a visit," Wily said aloud.

He drove to the old docks, taking back streets and side roads, so he would know if he was being followed. When he got there, a sign pointed left to Gallery Nouvelle. But shortly after Wily turned left, a strange thing happened – the road ran out.

Wily looked in front of him. Gallery Nouvelle seemed to be on an island linked to the mainland by a moveable bridge. The bridge was up and a gruff-looking goat was standing in front of it.

Who would want to stop anyone getting to their gallery? Wily thought to himself.

He considered swimming across to the island, but the water looked murky and the current seemed strong. Then he glanced down at his Vespa and remembered – it couldn't just fly...

The goat heard the splash and glanced round. But Wily and his Vespa had already vanished. As soon as it hit the water, a Perspex bubble shot out of the front, the screen on the handlebars flipped over and a giant propeller popped out of the back. The Vespa had become a submarine.

Wily steered it carefully towards the island. When he got close, he pressed a blue button on the dashboard and a periscope whirred up from the handlebars.

It was early evening now. As Wily peered through the periscope, he could see no signs of life in the gallery. All the lights were off, and all the doors and windows were closed.

He drove the Vespa towards the edge of the island and, just before he hit dry land, he pressed a button. The Vespa crunched and clanked, rising up through the water, and Wily emerged riding a scooter again, as if he'd never been underwater at all.

The detective took a torch out of the Vespa's top box and walked towards the gallery. He glanced around, looking for security guards. There didn't seem to be any – just a high fence with barbed wire along the top.

Wily bit through the fencing with one huge chomp of his sharp teeth and crawled through the hole he had made. Then he slunk across to the gallery.

The door was locked but, with the help of a hairpin from his inside pocket, he picked the lock in less than three seconds.

"A personal best," he muttered.

Once inside, Wily turned on his torch. He could see square shapes on each of the walls. He guessed they were paintings. He could see weird objects in the middle of the floor. He guessed they were pieces of sculpture.

Now all he had to do was find the Kandogski. Wily moved across to the nearest wall and shone his torch on the first square shape. Strange. It wasn't a painting at all. In fact, it seemed to be a signed photograph of the French football team. He shone his torch on the next square. But that wasn't a painting, either. It was a calendar with a different racing car for each month. The next square was a list of names on a whiteboard.

Wily shone his torch round the entire room and realized that this wasn't an art gallery. The shapes he had seen were not paintings and sculptures. They were car engines and noticeboards and workbenches and spanners and screwdrivers and tyres.

This was a garage.

Why would anyone send a painting to a garage? And why was this garage on an island behind a barbed-wire fence?

Wily looked around for other clues. He shone his torch on the workbench and saw a note. It was written in the same handwriting that he had seen on the photo of his old classmates:

You have the first two. Dimitri is sending you the third. I will send the fourth from Moscow tonight. You need six to build.

"You have the first two," Wily murmured. "That must mean the first two paintings. So they're here. Somewhere."

The detective looked around the garage again and saw a large shape under a brown cloth.

He crossed the room and lifted up the cloth. There were two paintings underneath. They were in the same unusual style as Suzie La Pooch's Kandogski.

Wily quickly took a
photo and emailed it to
Albert. He needed to think.
He needed to think hard.
Instead, the phone went.
The detective froze.
Mounted on the wall was
a large red telephone. He glanced
round – was there a guard on duty? Was
someone going to emerge, half asleep,
from a side room?

After five rings, nobody had appeared.
Wily went over and picked up the phone.
He held his mobile against the receiver, so he
could record the whole conversation.

There was silence on the other end
of the line.

Putting on his best French accent, Wily
said, "*Bonjour!*"

There was more silence. Then a voice said, "Paris will not work."

The voice had been put through a scrambler – it was impossible to work out the age or gender of who was talking.

Dimitri has messed up and Wily Fox is sniffing around. Dimitri is heading to Moscow. Send the paintings back. We will try Madrid instead.

There was a click and the line went dead.

Wily put the phone back on the hook. This case was becoming stranger by the second. Then his mobile buzzed. It was Suzie.

"Wily," she said. "I've just been arrested."

THE MYSTERIOUS
MOSCOW MISSION

"OK, Suzie," said Wily, "tell me exactly what happened."

"It's that Julius Hound," said Suzie. "He says he's contacted the Russian branch of PSSST. *And* he says Kandogski's not a real painter."

"Er, that's probably true, I'm afraid," said Wily.

"Of course he's real," said Suzie.

"I mean, the painting's real, isn't it? If not, who painted it? A machine?"

That made Wily pause and think for a second. Then he said, "Even if Kandogski isn't real, why should Julius arrest you?"

"He claims I knew all along," said Suzie. "That I bought the painting so I could give Dimitri lots of money. He thinks I'm smuggling something, or hiding something, or who knows what. He keeps saying, 'Tell me everything'. But there's nothing to tell. And now I'm in this ghastly prison cell."

"I'm going to get you out, Suzie," said Wily. "But first I have to go to Moscow."

"Moscow?"

"I'm in a garage down by the old docks. There's a note here that says a fourth painting was coming from Moscow tonight. That's also where Dimitri's going. So that's where I'm heading."

"Oh no, you're not," said a voice behind him.

The lights came on. Wily turned round slowly and put his phone back in his pocket. The gruff-looking goat from the bridge and a sinister-looking weasel were standing in front of him. They were both holding truncheons.

Wily had to think fast. "At last!" he exclaimed. "Some service! I've been waiting here for SIX HOURS!"

The goat and the weasel looked at each other. "Nice try, pal," said the weasel.

"I brought in my scooter for a service TWO WEEKS AGO. And you said it would be ready the NEXT DAY. So, where is it?" Wily demanded.

"Er, this is not a regular garage, Monsieur," said the goat.

"You're telling me!" said Wily. "I left my scooter out there on the grass. And I bet it's still there! I bet you haven't even *moved* it – let alone fixed it!"

He marched out of the door, pushing the goat and the weasel out of the way.

"Hold it one second," said the weasel suspiciously.

Wily reached the fence, pushed open the gate and strode over to where he had left the Vespa. The goat and the weasel scuttled along behind him, muttering to each other.

"Just as I told you," said Wily, pointing to the scooter. "And I bet it's still broken!"

He got on to the Vespa, flicked on the turbo thrusters, put it in flight mode and revved the engine.

A grin spread across his face. "You *have* fixed it!" he whooped.

Wily whizzed up into the air and within a few seconds the pair were just specks below him. A minute later, he was zooming across the French capital.

Wily looked at the Vespa's petrol gauge. Enough to get him to Moscow. More or less. He brought Albert up on the screen.

"Ah, Wily," said Albert. He was surrounded by pots of ink. "Glad you phoned. Made some progress. Analyzed the handwriting on that photo you sent. But couldn't find writing samples of everyone in the picture."

"That doesn't sound like progress," said Wily, steering the Vespa gently to the left.

"Yes, but looking at the stroke, length, angle and slant of the handwriting, I was able to reconstruct the paw of the animal that wrote it. It's definitely a fox."

"A fox? Are you sure?"

"Positive," said Albert.

Wily took out the photo and a pen and crossed off everyone that wasn't a fox.

It left three animals – Frankie Furlong, Vicky Vixen and Sandy Swift-Fox. None of them had seemed like potential criminals back in detective school.

"OK," said Wily, "I'm sending you a sound file. Scrambled. It's the person who's behind all this. See if you can find out anything about them."

"Will do," said Albert.

Wily thanked Albert and flipped the screen over, revealing the Vespa's control panel. He pressed the "Autopilot" button.

A message appeared on screen: Location?

Wily entered: Moscow, Russia.

The Vespa's controls jerked out of Wily's hand and the vehicle began to fly itself. Wily's seat whirred backwards and turned into a bed, a roof popped out and a blanket appeared from a compartment. The detective lay back and started thinking.

What was *really* going on with this case? Three paintings by a painter that didn't appear to exist. A Russian art dealer sending paintings to a garage.

And controlling it all, a fox – a fox who seemed to have a connection to Wily.

A name popped into Wily's head, but before he could remember it clearly, he fell fast asleep.

Wily was jolted awake three hours later by a spluttering noise. The detective sat bolt upright and saw that the petrol gauge was flashing. He peered through the glass and saw Moscow beneath him.

The Vespa was trying to regain height, but it kept jerking downwards. There was only one thing for it – Wily had to bail out.

He opened the top box of the Vespa – quickly trying to work out what to take with him. He packed his notepad, his magnifying glass and his night-vision goggles. Then he saw a tuft of brown fur poking out from under the first-aid box.

Wily remembered his race up the Eiffel Tower. He had chased the wolf and pulled off his bear costume. Without thinking, he must have hung on to the costume as he fell through the air. And, here it was, still in the Vespa.

The detective put it on. It fitted him perfectly.

The Vespa juddered and lurched. Wily tapped a blue button on the control panel. A message appeared:

`Are you sure you want to eject?`

The Vespa lurched and then started to drop through the sky.

Wily tapped the **YES** button.

The seat rocketed out of the top of the Vespa. After shooting a hundred metres through the air, a parachute mushroomed out.

Slowly, steadily, Wily glided down towards Moscow.

But he didn't look like Wily. As far as Russia was concerned, Dimitri Gottabottomitch was back in town. There was only one problem – now there would be two Dimitris in the capital.

"This town ain't big enough for the both of us," Wily murmured.

DIMITRI'S DOUBLE TROUBLE

Wily landed in the middle of Red Square.
He looked around and saw ice glinting and
twinkling. Then he realized it wasn't ice. It was
steel. Thirty soldiers were surrounding him,
pointing rifles at his nose.

The detective stood up and brushed the
snow from his bear costume. He tried to
remember the Russian he had learned three
years ago when he had gone undercover in
the Russian Mafia and solved "The Case of the
Kidnapped Cosmonaut".

A Russian phrase popped into his head. "Don't you know who I am?" he said.

The soldiers glanced at each other but didn't move.

"I am Dimitri Gottabottomitch," Wily declared.

One of the soldiers whispered, "He's friends with the president."

"Take me to my gallery," said Wily.

"Where did he come from?" growled one of the older soldiers, looking up at the sky.

"I came from the Kremlin. On a top-secret mission from the president. Take me to my gallery or I'll get you all posted to Siberia," he said.

The soldiers looked at each other. A younger soldier seemed to take charge.

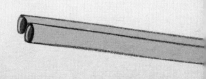

"Put him in a taxi. I don't fancy winter in Siberia."

Two soldiers escorted him to a taxi rank on the edge of Red Square and helped him into the first cab.

"Morning, Mr Gottabottomitch," said the driver. "Your gallery, I assume?"

Wily made the bear suit nod.

"Right you are, sir," said the driver.

They reached the gallery in about twenty minutes.

A wolf scuttled over, paid the driver and helped Wily out.

"Back already, boss," he said.

Wily made the bear suit nod once more. Then he walked quickly through the front doors.

"Oscar's nearly finished if you want to check on the painting," the wolf said, hovering at the detective's side.

Wily nodded for a third time and followed the wolf down a corridor. They walked past a showroom full of pictures by famous painters. Then they reached a thick security door with a fingerprint reader next to it.

Wily lifted up the paw of the costume, and placed it on the sensor.

The sensor flashed red. Of course it did. A costume could not imitate Dimitri's fingerprints.

Wily froze for a second and then put his paw back down angrily.

The reader flashed red again.

"Stupid thing," growled the wolf, and put his own paw on it.

The door hissed open.

"There you go, boss," he said and headed back down the corridor, leaving Wily alone.

Wily found himself in a large white room full of paintbrushes, plaster moulds, blank canvases and empty paint pots.

In the middle of the room, an otter was standing in front of a strange painting, chained to the floor by his ankles. The painting looked like this:

The otter turned round. "Almost finished," he said. "Just this final loop here to do."

Wily looked again at the otter's chains and made a quick decision.

He climbed out of the costume.

"Have you come to d-do me in?" the otter stammered, backing away.

Wily started to gnaw and chew on the otter's chains with his sharp teeth.

"Here to help," he said. "Now, tell me what's going on..."

The otter looked relieved. "I don't really know," he said. "I'm just an artist. Oscar Otter. I sold a few paintings to Dimitri last year. All abstract – a bit like this one. Then about three months ago, I got woken by a loud knock on the door, someone put a bag over my head and the next thing I know, I'm chained up here."

Wily couldn't get through the manacles with his teeth so he tried pulling them.

"Carry on," he grunted.

"I have to copy these strange pictures," the otter said. "I only get one at a time, so I never see them together. When they're given to me, they're just sketches – scraps of paper, torn round the edges. I have to turn them into paintings like this one. The thing is, a lot of them are the same. I've done this one at least twice before."

Wily stopped yanking for a second. "Say that again?"

"I've done this one before," the otter repeated.

Wily stopped to think. He took a picture of the painting, then he reached into his pocket and pulled out his college photo.

"Have you seen any of these foxes before?"

The otter stared for a few seconds and then shook his head.

"There was a vixen that brought me a fish once. I do like fish…"

"But it wasn't this vixen here?" Wily pointed out Vicky Vixen.

"No, she had light-brown fur. Hang on, I think I sketched her just after she left. I hide all my sketches under that concrete slab there. Lift it up and I'll show you."

Wily stepped forward and started to lift up the slab. A split second later, there was a loud…

Dimitri was standing in the doorway. Behind him stood the two wolves that Wily had met in Paris.

"We're doomed," the otter wailed, curling up behind his painting.

"Fast work, Wily Fox. I'd hoped you were still at the bottom of the Eiffel Tower, where we left you," growled Dimitri.

"Paint fight!" Wily shouted, letting the slab fall.

He picked up a tin of red paint and flung it at Dimitri, covering him from head to foot.

One of the wolves stepped forward and Wily threw a tin of blue paint at him. The wolf stopped in his tracks, wiping the paint out of his eyes and ears.

The other wolf picked up a tin of yellow paint and threw it at Wily.

Wily held his arms out wide, allowing himself to be covered. Then he grabbed two more paint pots from

behind the canvas, and handed one to the otter.

"Throw the paint as hard as you can," he said.

For the next two minutes, paint flew everywhere until everyone was sticky, spluttering and multicoloured.

"Get him!" shouted Dimitri.

But now it wasn't clear who was a wolf and who was a fox.

"OK, boss," Wily said in his best Russian accent, and jumped on one of the wolves. The other wolf joined in. Then Wily stepped away and let the two wolves roll around in the paint, kicking and thrashing about, until they had knocked each other out.

"Idiots!" roared Dimitri, and started throwing empty paint tins at Wily.

The detective jumped left and right, dodging Dimitri's missiles.

"Missed!" exclaimed Wily.

Then he grabbed the painting that the otter had been working on, and held it in front of him. The paint tin hit the canvas. The canvas stretched backwards, like a huge trampoline. Then the tin came rocketing back, towards Dimitri.

It hit the bear on the nose, sending him flying. Dimitri reeled and staggered, pulling things over and knocking things sideways. Eventually he ended up underneath a huge pile of easels, paintbrushes, cloths and buckets.

Wily grabbed some rope from a side table and tied up Dimitri. Then he tied up the two wolves.

After that, he turned round to check on the otter. But one of the paint tins had broken his chains, and the artist was nowhere to be seen.

Looks like he's an escape artist, too, thought Wily.

Now what had the otter said? He had drawn a picture of the fox that was behind all this and hidden it under a slab. Wily lifted up the slab. Underneath, he found a folded piece of paper. He opened it and saw this:

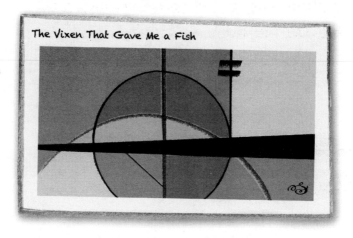

The Vixen That Gave Me a Fish

Oh no! It was in the same style as the otter's other paintings – a mass of weird shapes. It would have been Wily's best clue yet, but it was no use at all. And the otter was gone so he couldn't ask him any more questions.

He raced around the room, searching for other clues. And then he spotted it. The otter had written something on the back of the canvas he had been working on:

TO THE FOX WHO RESCUED ME. IF YOU EVER NEED MY HELP, CALL THIS NUMBER: 011 222 333.

Wily would look for the otter later. Once he had found the vixen, the otter could help to identify her.

As the detective folded up the piece of paper, something started to buzz under the pile of easels and cloths and buckets.

Dimitri's phone was under there.

WILY GETS ICED

Wily pulled Dimitri's phone out from under the pile. He had a new message:

MEET ME ON THE RIVER MOSKVA IN ONE HOUR. THERE IS A NEW PLAN FOR THE FINAL PAINTINGS.

This was a bit of luck. The message could only be from one person – the fox who was behind everything. The detective's nose twitched, his ears pricked up and his cheeks tingled.

"Wily Fox," he murmured, "solving crime in record time."

He pulled out his phone and called Albert. But it went through to voicemail:

I'm sorry. I'm not able to answer your call at the moment. Please leave a message after the controlled explosion.

There was a sound effect of an explosion…

That was strange. Albert always answered.

Wily decided to call Suzie La Pooch instead. He needed to give her an update and tell her she'd soon be free. He phoned Sybil Squirrel's number at PSSST. Julius wouldn't let him talk to Suzie, but Sybil might.

But there was another recorded message:

Sorry, there's nobody in the PSSST office to take your call. Please leave a message after the police siren.

NEE-NAW-NEE-NAW, went the sound effect.

That was even stranger. There was always someone in the PSSST offices.

"You're out of your depth, Fox," said a voice behind him.

Wily turned round and saw that a groggy-looking Dimitri, still bound hand and foot, had propped himself up against the wall.

"Oh yeah," said Wily. "Why's that?"

"You will never beat her," said Dimitri. "She sees everything, and knows everything."

"Who? Who are you talking about?"

Dimitri shook his head.

Wily pulled out the old college photo. "It's her, isn't it? Vicky Vixen?"

"She's not in the photo," said Dimitri, "but she's there just the same."

"What do you mean?"

"You're the detective. You work it out." Dimitri closed his eyes.

Wily shook him, but the bear had passed out again.

The detective tried to think. Six paintings. Painted over and over again. Sent to garages not galleries. And a fox that wasn't there. He looked at the paintings on his phone again.

Hmm. Maybe he *was* out of his depth. But it was time to go. Whoever he was about to meet on the River Moskva – she would have the answers. He put on the bear costume and left the studio.

The River Moskva was frozen and covered with snow. Everywhere there were ice skaters in fur coats and hats, young animals pulling each other along on sledges and old donkeys in kiosks selling hot coffee and soup.

Wily scanned the river for any sign of a vixen. Nothing. She was late.

A couple of seconds later, a group of ice skaters parted to reveal a tall, elegant fox in dark glasses and a scarf tied, bandit-style, around her muzzle. She had a large briefcase in one paw. Ice skates glinted on her feet.

The fox was about twenty metres away. She was staring at Wily the bear. There was no expression on her face. This wasn't Vicky Vixen.

Wily breathed in, trying to catch the fox's scent. Across the ice, the other fox was also breathing in, and she had caught Wily's. Her blank expression turned to one of surprise, then anger. She spun round and sped off.

Wily was out of the bear costume in seconds. He ran on to the ice, skidding in all directions. He was never going to catch up with the fox at this rate. He needed to find ice skates or skis or a sledge – or anything but his paws.

Then he heard a growling sound behind him and a voice declared, "It can turn into a snowmobile, too."

"Albert?" Wily gasped.

The mole was riding the Vespa, which now had two giant skis under its chassis.

"When the Vespa went down over Moscow, it sent out a distress call," Albert explained. "I came out here to repair it."

"But how did you get here so fast?"

"Rocket socks," he said, glancing at his feet. "Still need some work. Should be ready for your next case. Anyway, after I fixed your bike, I locked on to your mobile signal."

Wily grinned. "Clever. Now budge over – I'm driving."

Albert shuffled back and Wily leaped on. They gave chase and within moments they were closing in on the fox.

She was swerving between groups of skaters, leaping over sledges and looping around holes in the ice.

Albert was taking photos of her and trying to analyze them.

"She's not showing up in any databases," he said.

"Don't worry," said Wily. "We'll soon catch her and then we'll know everything."

But the fox sped up, heading downstream where the ice was thinner.

Wily also picked up speed, making skaters leap out of the way.

"Take over," he told Albert, "and get as close as you can."

The mole grabbed the handlebars and steered the Vespa towards the vixen. Wily stood up behind him, getting ready to jump.

The vixen glanced over her shoulder and growled.

Wily jumped towards her, but as he did so, she whacked him with her briefcase. And Wily – in a reflex action – grabbed it.

The vixen tugged.

Wily tugged.

The vixen tugged harder.

The briefcase sprang open, spilling its contents over the ice. Wily saw six paintings, all in the style of Kandogski. The vixen looked down at the pictures and then up at Wily. She growled before speeding off, leaving them on the ice.

"Albert!" Wily called.

But the mole was fifty metres away, turning the Vespa in a wide arc.

Wily tried to stand up, but the ice was too slippery. He saw the empty briefcase and had an idea. Two seconds later, he was pushing himself along the ice with his arms, using the briefcase as a sledge.

"Get the paintings! I'll chase the fox!" he yelled to Albert.

Within moments, Wily had nearly caught up with the vixen again. She snarled and went faster, but the detective pushed even harder and sped up, too. As they headed downstream,

Wily could see that the ice was getting thinner. It groaned and crackled beneath him.

Wily was within a metre of the vixen now. He tried to grab her feet, her arms, her tail. She swerved out of the way, narrowly avoiding a large crack in the ice.

"Who are you?" Wily muttered.

The vixen turned round, as if she'd heard his question.

"The one that got away," she said in a low voice.

She pulled up a scuba mask from around her neck then she dived through a crack in the ice and vanished.

Wily slammed down with his fists and brought the briefcase to a stop by the hole. He peered into the icy water. A split second later, an arm emerged from the hole and pulled him under.

JULIUS CHILLS OUT

The water was freezing cold. Wily felt himself go stiff. At the same time, he felt two paws close around his neck. Wily opened his eyes but everything was blurry. He could only see the outline of a fox's head and, above him, thick ice. He started to struggle but the vixen wasn't letting go.

Quickly, he thought about what was in his pocket. No weapons, just his magnifying glass, his notepad (now soggy) and his phone.

His phone. His phone was waterproof,

bombproof, everything proof. It would still work.

As the vixen gripped tightly to his throat, Wily managed to move his paw into his pocket and grab his phone. He was holding his breath but he knew he couldn't last too much longer. With his thumb, he switched his phone to camera mode. He moved it slowly up, in between the arms that were choking him, and started taking pictures.

FLASH

FLASH

FLASH

Even underwater, the light was blinding. Realizing what was happening, the vixen let go and tried to grab the phone.

Which was exactly what Wily wanted. The detective pressed a small blue button on the back of the phone. All of Albert's gadgets had this button. It was meant as a last resort, but this *was* a last resort.

These words appeared on the phone's screen:

THIS DEVICE WILL
SELF-DESTRUCT
IN TEN SECONDS.

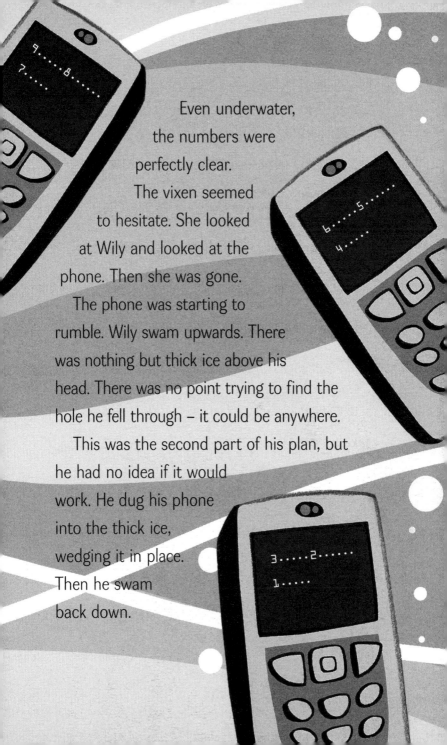

Even underwater, the numbers were perfectly clear.

The vixen seemed to hesitate. She looked at Wily and looked at the phone. Then she was gone.

The phone was starting to rumble. Wily swam upwards. There was nothing but thick ice above his head. There was no point trying to find the hole he fell through – it could be anywhere.

This was the second part of his plan, but he had no idea if it would work. He dug his phone into the thick ice, wedging it in place. Then he swam back down.

Wily was about ten metres below the surface when the phone exploded, blasting a huge hole in the ice. The explosion spun him round and round, but he was still conscious. Just.

The detective swam to the surface as fast as he could. He could feel the air in his lungs running out. Black blobs appeared in front of his eyes. He was about to pass out, when his head emerged above the water. He took a gigantic breath and his strength flooded back.

"Albert!" he gasped.

Wily looked around but all he could see was smoke from the explosion. Then a second later, the Vespa's headlamp appeared through the cloud and Albert was beside him.

"Did you catch her?" he asked.

"No, but I know who she is," Wily smiled, climbing out. "It's like Dimitri said – she's not in the picture, but she's there all the same."

Wily pulled the photograph out of his pocket. It was wet but otherwise undamaged.

"You mean she's hiding behind one of those trees?" said Albert.

Wily shook his head. "Who does the photo belong to?"

Albert thought for a second and smiled. "The person who took it," he said.

"That's why she's not in the photo," said Wily.

"Her name is Klara, and she's the cleverest fox I've ever met. When I was in the river, I saw the outline of her face."

"But what is she doing – and why?" asked Albert.

"Let's get out of here," said Wily, "and I'll explain."

Albert drove the Vespa towards the shore.

"Klara was brilliant," said Wily, as they drove along. "Came top in every exam we took. But she was also superstitious. She had this lucky mascot called Captain Snuggles. He was a small fluffy puffin with a missing eye – she'd had it since childhood. Wherever she went, Captain Snuggles went, too. Every exam, Captain Snuggles was there, sitting on the desk in front of her."

"So she thought the puffin brought her good luck?"

"Exactly. Then one day, she lost him. Maybe someone stole it as a prank – we never found out. Anyway, she went crazy. Phoned the police. Screamed at them. Insisted they find it. Of course they didn't take her seriously. It was a soft toy, after all. But from that day, everything changed. Klara stopped working. She came bottom in every exam. Started picking fights with the rest of us. Picked fights with the teachers, too. A couple of months later, she was expelled."

"Are you saying she's a criminal mastermind because of a *fluffy puffin*?" said Albert.

"That's what started it," said Wily. "But we have to work out what's happened since then. And what she's up to now. Did you pick up the paintings?"

Albert nodded.

"Then let's go somewhere quiet and look at what we've got," said Wily.

Albert pulled in by the jetty at the bottom of Red Square. Beside them, other animals were tying up sledges or unclipping their skis.

They parked the Vespa and started to walk towards the palace. They were crossing Red Square when they heard a familiar voice.

"Hold it right there!"

Wily looked up and saw Julius Hound, Sybil Squirrel and fifteen PSSST agents blocking their path.

"Julius … for goodness' sake…?" Wily stammered.

The PSSST agents were all holding snowballs.

"Give up, Wily," Sybil pleaded. "Let's sort this out."

"I am sorting it out," said Wily.

"We know you're involved, Wily Fox," said Julius. "We tracked down Dimitri to a garage in Paris. Your paw prints were all over it. Then we investigated Dimitri's gallery here in Moscow. Your paw prints were everywhere, too."

"That's because I've been *investigating* the case," said Wily. "Listen, Julius, the villain behind this is somebody called Klara Kraftypants. I was at detective school with her. These paintings here are all the evidence I need to find her and get to the bottom of what her evil scheme is."

"Here's what I think of your evidence," said Julius. He turned to his agents. "Now, FIRE!"

The agents began pelting them with snowballs. Wily quickly grabbed Albert and rolled out of the way, ducking behind a snowdrift.

"OK, Albert," he said. "You roll 'em and I'll chuck 'em."

The mole immediately started rolling
snowballs and lining them up next to the fox's
feet. Wily threw his first snowball, which hit a
junior sergeant on the nose.

The agents threw again – snowballs landed
to the left and right of Wily and Albert, but the
snowdrift stopped any direct hits.

Wily poked his head over the top of the drift and a huge snowball flew between his ears.

"Julius!" Wily called out. "Klara is planning something big. We're wasting time fighting like this."

Julius's reply was another snowball, followed by a dozen more from his agents. Their snowballs started to knock lumps out of the top of the snowdrift.

"We're losing our shield, Albert," said Wily. "Can you roll any faster?"

But Albert was running out of breath.

"Let me take another look at their position," said Wily.

He poked his head out from behind the snowdrift again and a giant snowball caught him on the cheek.

"Give up yet?" barked Julius.

"Right," said Wily, kneeling down next to Albert.

"I've got a plan. They're backed up against the palace wall. There's a giant blanket of snow balanced on the roof." He whispered something into Albert's ear. Albert frowned and then nodded.

"Good," said Wily.

He rolled Albert around in the snow until he had made a giant snowball. Then, using all his strength, the detective picked up his Albert-snowball and flung it at the palace roof. It flew through the air, soaring over the PSSST agents' heads.

"Not even close!" growled Julius.

The Albert-snowball landed on top of the palace roof, just as Wily had planned. The mole burst out and began kicking and pushing the snow on the roof.

There was a rumbling noise and Julius glanced up. Just as he realized what was happening, a huge avalanche of snow rolled down from the roof, burying the bulldog and his agents in a two-metre-deep snowdrift.

"Chill-out time!" laughed Wily.

SOLVING CRIME IN RECORD TIME

Albert slid off the roof and rejoined Wily. The PSSST agents were all scrabbling through the mound of snow, trying to get out. Wily and Albert were about to leave Red Square and continue their hunt for Klara Kraftypants when Sybil Squirrel confronted them.

"I'm sorry, Wily," she said, "but I'm going to have to take you in."

"Managed to avoid the avalanche, eh?" said Wily.

"Saw what you were planning a mile off,"

said Sybil. "Poor Albert – you're always chucking him around."

"Oh, I don't mind," said Albert, rubbing his back. "I quite like it, really."

"Look, Sybil, let me tell you what I know," said Wily. "And then you can decide whether to arrest us. Come on, before your boss gets out of there."

Sybil glanced at the pile of snow covering Julius. "OK," she said, "but this better be good or he'll arrest me, too."

Wily, Albert and Sybil crossed Red Square, ducked inside a cafe and found a table near the back. Wily pulled out Klara's paintings. There were six in total.

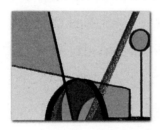 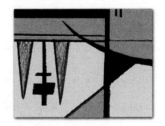

 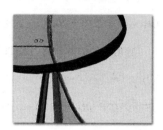

"These belong to Klara Kraftypants," Wily explained. He told Sybil who Klara was and how he knew her.

"She's been sending sketches to Dimitri Gottabottomitch," he continued. "Dimitri locked up a young artist – Oscar Otter – at his gallery here in Moscow, and has been forcing him to turn the sketches into these paintings. Dimitri then smuggled the paintings abroad. They look like ordinary abstract paintings, so nobody suspects anything. The paintings end up in garages and workshops – to make what, I don't know. But there are always six. And my hunch is that he's not just sent them to Paris – they've gone to other places, too."

"So how did Suzie La Pooch get one?" Sybil asked.

"Total mistake," said Wily. "One of the paintings ended up in Dimitri's Paris gallery. Suzie saw it and fell in love with it. Bought it on the spot. The gallery assistant didn't realize it should have been sent to the Gallery Nouvelle."

"So where is Klara now?" Sybil asked.

"Half an hour ago, she was here in Moscow, trying to drown me," said Wily. "I'm sure that the answer to everything – where she is and what she's doing – can be found in these paintings."

Sybil and Albert stared at the six paintings.

"Is that a radio mast?" Albert said, pointing at one of the long lines.

"I'm not sure," said Sybil. "It could be a map of somewhere?"

"Where, though?" Albert asked.

"I don't know," Sybil sighed. "It's a puzzle, all right."

Wily suddenly went very quiet and started shuffling the small paintings around.

"That's it," he murmured. "That's it!"

"What's it?" Albert asked.

"A puzzle, a puzzle," Wily muttered. "You said it was a puzzle, and that's exactly what it is."

Wily rotated the six paintings and slotted them back together.

"Oh no, this is bad," Albert muttered. "This is really, really bad."

"Why?" Sybil asked.

"That's a mega-torpedo," said Albert. "Fires a huge laser beam out of that gun barrel there. It's powerful enough to wipe out a whole city."

At that second, the waitress appeared – a young bandicoot in a white apron.

"Is one of you three Wily Fox?" she asked.

Wily glanced up. "Who's asking?"

The waitress handed him a note. "She said you'd know who it was from."

Wily looked concerned.

I hope you're enjoying your coffee. Come to Apartment D in Block 17 in one hour or I will destroy this city. Make sure you are alone. Bring my paintings.

"Well, you can't go!" Albert exclaimed.

"Albert's right," said Sybil. "If she really is building these weapons, she's not going to think twice about killing you."

"I have to go – the city is at stake," said Wily. "I know Klara, remember. I can try to reason with her. And if that fails, I've got another idea. It involves an otter, some cloth fabric and running around at high speed. But I'll need your help to make it work."

Albert and Sybil looked at each other.

"Count me in," said Albert.

"Me, too," said Sybil. "What's the plan?"

Twenty minutes later, Wily was walking up the stairs towards Apartment D in Block 17.

The detective knocked on the door of the apartment and waited. There was no answer so he tried the handle. The door was unlocked so he pushed it open.

Wily found himself in some kind of reception area. There was a door with frosted glass at one end of the room. Next to the door was a chair. On the wall opposite there were two paintings, both by famous painters: one showed a frog catching a fly, the other was of a weasel chasing a rabbit. Piped music was coming from a speaker somewhere.

It seemed to be a conventional office in an ordinary apartment block. Was this really Klara's headquarters?

Wily tried the door with frosted glass but it was locked. He would have to wait.

The detective sat on the chair next to the door. At once, he knew he'd made a mistake. He heard a loud click. Leather cords whipped round his body and legs, pinning him to the spot. Then the ground gave way and he was falling.

Wily tried to stay calm but within a couple of seconds, he was yelling. He looked down and saw the ground approaching fast. Then the chair appeared, somehow, to slow down and it dropped with a clunk on to a stone floor.

The detective found himself looking down the nose of a gigantic metal mega-torpedo.

"Hello, Wily," said a voice by his shoulder.
Klara walked round to face him.

"I knew you'd come," she said. "I only had to mention that I'd blow up the city, and off you trot, trying to stop me."

Klara was tall and slender with narrow green eyes. She was holding a remote control in her paw. She leaned over and grabbed the paintings from Wily's paw.

"Mine, I believe," she said. "Now it's time to try out my new toy."

"Klara, let's talk about this," said Wily.

"We *are* going to talk," said Klara. "I'm going to tell you all about my plan for world domination. I've got five of these beauties. One here and four others in Rio, Sydney, New York and Beijing. The one in Paris would have been number six. Until *you* spoiled things."

Wily stared up at the torpedo that was

pointing at his snout. "I'll fix things," he said. "Let me work for you."

"Nice try, Wily," said Klara. "You're forgetting that we went to detective school together. 'Pretending you're on the villain's side' – we learned that in the first week! No, I'm now going to test setting one on my mega-torpedo. This will blow up you and part of the wall behind you, but leave everything else intact."

Wily looked at Klara and up at the underground vault that he was in. He knew his only chance was to keep Klara talking and hope his back-up plan would work.

"Why do you need six of them? Isn't one enough?" he asked.

Klara paused. "Oh, now we're on to week two. 'Buy yourself time by flattering the villain with questions about their plan.'

This is why I *hated* detective school. Not challenging enough."

"OK, I'll tell *you*, then," said Wily. "If you link six together, you give yourself a weapon capable of blowing up the whole world. Is that it?"

Klara blinked. "Very good, Wily Fox. If you point all six at the Earth's core, you can create a blast of energy strong enough to destroy the entire planet."

"That's why you've been so careful. Breaking the plans into six sketches. Using paintings to smuggle them."

Klara grinned. "I couldn't risk being stopped until I had all six. Other ways of transporting the plans were all problematic. Put them in a suitcase? I get searched at customs all the time. Email them? The government scans everything I send. But I've always collected paintings.

And I noticed that no customs official ever looks at the paintings I buy. When I met Dimitri, the rest of my plan fell into place."

As Klara talked, Wily was fumbling in his pockets. It was hard because his paws were strapped to his sides, but eventually he managed to grab his magnifying glass.

"Then Suzie La Pooch messed that up," said Wily.

"Too right," said Klara. "When she got hold of that painting, things spiralled out of control. Dimitri was too heavy-handed and I KNEW Suzie would contact you. What with your so-called 'reputation' for 'helping' other animals. I sent Dimitri a photo – telling him to look out for you – but he messed that up, too. I'm SURROUNDED by bunglers."

Wily lowered the magnifying glass on to his lap. "But why are you doing this, Klara?" he asked.

You used to be … well … a *laugh*."

"I still am," she said. "I just find different things funny." Klara pressed a button on her remote control. "Goodbye, Wily," she chuckled.

The mega-torpedo started to shudder and hum.

Wily managed to twist his arm so that the magnifying glass was angled down by his knees.

"What's it all for?" he shouted over the noise of the mega-torpedo. "Money? Fame? Power?"

"No," said Klara. "It's worse than that – I actually *want* to destroy the world. And when you're out of the way, I'll build my sixth mega-torpedo in Madrid and finish the job."

"But you'll die as well!" protested Wily.

"I don't care about that," said Klara. "I haven't since one of you lot stole Captain Snuggles and left me alone in the world. Now I want to take every animal down with me."

Klara pressed another button on her remote control. "Starting with you."

A huge blast of energy shot out of the end of the mega-torpedo. But Wily's idea worked. He'd hoped his magnifying glass would change the path of the laser beam. And it did – the laser hit the glass and curved round, blasting apart the leather straps that tied his legs to the chair.

Wily leaped up and ran, the chair still strapped to his back.

It took Klara a couple of seconds to realize what had happened. She tapped frantically on her remote control, growling and snarling. The mega-torpedo swivelled round and kept blasting at Wily, taking chunks out of the walls and floor.

Wily was darting from left to right, not really knowing where he was going, trying to wriggle free of the chair.

"Fire! Fire!" shouted Klara.

Wily thought about Albert and Sybil. Maybe his other plan would work, but at this rate he might not live to see it.

"Fire!" shouted Klara again, and a blast of purple fire whistled past Wily's head.

In desperation, he tried to run behind the mega-torpedo, but the chair on his back shifted round and tripped him up. As he fell to the floor, he could hear the mega-torpedo spinning round.

"Fire!" said Klara.

"Wait!" said a voice above them.

The mega-torpedo had been making so much noise that they hadn't heard the Vespa tunnelling through the earth above Klara's underground vault.

The scooter dropped through the hole and landed on the ground with a crunch.

Sybil Squirrel was driving it. Albert was hanging on to the back. He was holding a fluffy puffin in his right paw. He raised it into the air like a trophy.

"C-c-captain S-snuggles," stammered Klara.

"That's right," said Sybil. "And if you don't let Wily go, we'll rip him to shreds."

"H-how? Wh-where?" Klara stammered.

"We went back to your detective school and searched every room," said Albert. "He was stuffed behind a locker in Room 2C."

"My old room," said Klara. "Let me see his eye."

Sybil held up the soft toy and the vixen stared at its face. Its eye was hanging by a thread.

"It's him," Klara whispered.

"Now, let Wily go and hand yourself in," said Sybil.

"Let me cuddle him first," Klara pleaded. "Just for a second."

Wily had clambered to his feet and wriggled free from his bonds.

"No," he said. "First, you will shut down your mega-torpedoes. Then you will give us a list of all of the animals that helped you put this plan into action. If you do as we ask, you can have Captain Snuggles back. Forever."

Klara paused for a second and looked down

at the remote control. She shrugged. "Who cares about a bunch of silly torpedoes?" She threw the remote at Wily.

The detective started tapping at the controls. The mega-torpedo in the centre of the room groaned and shut down.

Klara took a memory card out of her pocket. "Here are all my agents and their locations. Right, NOW can I have my puffin?"

"Handcuffs first," said Sybil.

Klara held out her paws and Sybil cuffed them. Then Albert gave Klara the soft toy.

A few seconds later, a squadron of PSSST agents came pouring into the vault. They abseiled down the shaft inside Apartment D, they leaped out of the hole that the Vespa had made, they sprang out of every door and hatch.

Julius Hound led the charge.

"We got reports of explosions under this building," said Julius. "What in heaven's name is going on?"

"Hello, Sarge," said Sybil. "I was just about to radio you. We've solved the Painting Plot. The mega-torpedoes have been shut down and the criminal is secure. It's another great day for PSSST."

Julius looked suspiciously at Wily and then at the deactivated mega-torpedo.

"Hmph," he said. "It does look like everything is under control. Stand down, everyone."

Sybil winked at Wily and led Klara out of the vault, surrounded by other PSSST agents.

"Congratulations, Julius," said Wily. "Sybil worked everything out. You've got a brilliant agent there."

"Hmph," said Julius again. "Well, she learned from the best. And it just goes to show – we don't need your help. Don't interfere with PSSST next time. Or EVER."

"I'll do my best," said Wily.

Julius followed his agents out of the vault.

Albert turned to Wily. "When do you think Klara will realize that the puffin is a fake?"

The vault was pierced by a sudden ear-splitting...

SCREAM!

"About now," said Wily.

Wily was standing in Suzie La Pooch's gallery in Paris, looking at two new paintings.

He heard the click of high-heeled shoes behind him and turned round.

"Do you like them, Mr Fox?" Suzie asked.

The first painting was of a frog catching a fly, the second was of a weasel chasing a rabbit.

"I'm sure I've seen them somewhere before," said Wily with a smile.

"When Klara was arrested, all her paintings were seized by the government," said Suzie. "I picked these up for next to nothing."

Wily nodded.

"I see it as fair compensation – for my week in prison," said Suzie.

Wily nodded again.

"So, Mr Fox, are you going to tell me how you did it?"

"Which part?" Wily asked.

"The last part," said Suzie. "When you were about to be blasted to smithereens by a mega-torpedo."

Wily smiled. "I had some help there. I knew about Klara's lucky mascot. Oscar Otter had told me I could contact him if I needed his help. I put the two together – a missing mascot and an expert forger."

"He could remake the fluffy puffin?" Suzie asked.

"He could try. He'd have art equipment – paint, fabric, stuffing, feathers. I knew Albert would be able to find the design online. I gave them a couple of extra details, like the fact it had one eye hanging out. Albert and Sybil whizzed across to the otter's studio and they made the puffin in ten minutes flat. It didn't have to be perfect. Just good enough to fool Klara for a minute or two."

"Hmm," said Suzie. "She's probably pretty angry right now."

Wily started to walk towards the door.

"Yes," he said, "but she's in Grimm Island Maximum Security Prison. And nobody's ever broken out of there. Actually, that's not strictly true. One animal has."

"Oh yes? Who?" asked Suzie.

"Me," said Wily, opening the door and walking out into the street.

He turned and smiled. "But that's another story."

COMING SOON...

FOX Investigates

A Whiff of Mystery

WILY FOX PI

SOLVING CRIME IN RECORD TIME!

· One family fortune

· A treasure map

· And a very special spider...

From the skyscrapers of New York to the villages of Peru, detective Wily Fox is on the trail of the *real* Simon Sheep, inheritor to a huge fortune. Someone has stolen Simon's identity, and it's up to Wily to prove the imposter is a fake. Can Wily solve the case of the missing millionaire before the villain hits the jackpot?

ABOUT THE AUTHOR

Adam Frost writes children's books full of jokes, animals, amazing gadgets – and ideally all three! When he was young, his favourite book was Roald Dahl's *Fantastic Mr Fox*, so writing about fantastic foxes all day is pretty much his dream job. His previous books include *Ralph the Magic Rabbit* and *Danny Danger and the Cosmic Remote*.

www.adam-frost.com